Don't Look In The Trees
Jason Nickey

BIBLIOBEARD
BOOKS

For Matthew Vaughn

A kick ass writer, an inspiration, and a good friend.

I've come to realize that the biggest problem anywhere in the world is that people's perceptions of reality are compulsively filtered through the screening mesh of what they want, and do not want, to be true.

-Travis Walton

Contents

Prologue

FRANK GRAVES ADJUSTED THE wire hanger that stuck out from the end of his broken TV antenna in an attempt to improve his reception. The black and white static on his screen resembled a snowstorm, occasionally giving way to show blurred characters from a syndicated sitcom.

Jesus, I need a new TV, he thought to himself, knowing that wouldn't make much of a difference. The cable companies didn't service the more rural areas of the county yet, and he didn't have the money for a satellite. *Hell,* he thought, *fucker probably wouldn't get good reception down here anyway.*

To Frank, it was a small price to pay for the solitude of the cabin, which he enjoyed immensely. He'd inherited his cabin, along with the one on the other end of the holler when his father had died ten years ago. He had grown up using them as a getaway for weekend hunting trips, but as he got older and his marriage grew sour, they became more of an escape from his wife Linda.

His little getaways didn't fool Linda, especially since, as time went on, he rarely returned with any kills. She knew he hadn't been cheating on her. "Frank is many things, most of them bad, but he's at least loyal," she would often say to people.

She knew he was just using the trips to get away from her, and she appreciated the break from him as well. Eventually, they both came to their senses and filed for divorce.

They ended up selling the house they shared shortly after. Linda took her half and moved into an apartment in town. Frank, on the other hand, took his half of the sale and moved into one of the cabins, even opting to retire a few years early to enjoy his solitude in the mountains.

He'd let his son Justin move into the other cabin just a few months ago after falling on some hard times. He'd wanted better for his son, but knew times were tough for a lot of people at the moment. He also appreciated having someone living in the other cabin to keep it from falling into disrepair.

Still fidgeting with the TV, he began wishing the two cabins were a bit closer to each other. If so, he could probably talk Justin into splitting the cost of a satellite dish.

Making no headway in getting the reception to come in any better, Frank switched the channel a few more times before getting frustrated and slapping the top of the console.

"Goddamn piece of shit!" he yelled to no one as he stood up and made his way to the kitchen to grab a beer from the fridge. He cracked open the can and took a big chug before setting it down on the coffee table and heading over to the bookshelf full of VHS tapes.

He perused the titles on his shelf, which were mostly movies recorded from before his divorce; back when he had cable. His collection was mostly action, westerns, and old war films, but he had a few horror movies and porno titles as well. As his eyes scanned the tapes, he let out a chuckle at some of the porno titles.

Been a while since I popped one of these in, he thought to himself. In truth, he hadn't watched any of his adult films in a while. He would never admit it to anyone, but his drive and stamina were not what they had once been.

He looked over the other tapes once more before settling on one called 'Busty Beach Bimbos'. "This'll do," he said with a laugh as he popped the tape in.

He turned the TV to channel three and plopped his ass on the couch, lighting a cigarette as he did so. As the movie began to play, and the scantily clad women began taking off what little clothes they had on, he steadily sipped on his beer. He chain smoked as he watched, letting each cigarette rest on his lips as he played with himself through his pants, only taking his hand off his member to occasionally flick his ash into the already overflowing ashtray.

He was about an hour into the tape and just about to whip out his member to partake in some self-gratification when the sight of lights outside his window pulled him out of his horny trance.

"Goddammit," he cried out as he stood up and made his way to the front window.

Looking outside, he expected to see a vehicle approaching, but all he saw was his front yard, illuminated by some light source coming from behind the cabin.

He stepped outside, walking backwards as soon as he was off of the porch. As he slowly continued to walk backwards, he stood in awe at the sight of lights coming down from the sky. They came down in streaks, almost like lightning, only stationary. They seemed to be pulsating. A chill ran down his spine as he noticed the humming sound that seemed to be surrounding him.

Is it coming from the lights? he wondered.

The more he paid attention, the more he realized that, outside of the hum from the lights and the barely audible moans coming from the women on his TV, there were no other sounds; no insects or critters that usually provided the nighttime soundtrack in the hollow.

The lights, along with the humming sound, eventually came to a stop. The stiffness in Frank's legs as he began to walk told him that he'd been standing there, staring at the lights for longer than he'd realized.

As he made his way back inside, he ignored the tape still playing on his screen and turned the TV to channel four. Unlike earlier, this time, the reception was better. The screen for the local news channel was locked on a 'Please be patient. The network is experiencing technical difficulties' banner.

With a confused look on his face, Frank reached to turn the dial to a different channel. He was caught off guard by the emergency alert tone coming loudly from the TV speaker. His jaw dropped as he read the message displayed on the screen, taken aback by the fact that it described exactly what he had seen outside. The last part of the message, warning viewers to remain inside and lock their doors, struck fear into his heart.

In a paranoid state, he began looking around the room, wondering if there could be something, or someone, outside right now. He screamed at the sound of the VHS tape reaching its end and ejecting from the player.

The emergency alert was now finished, and rather than going back to the technical difficulties banner, the network seemed to have shut down. The screen went to the snowy static, giving an almost strobe light effect to the dimly lit room.

Frank slowly inched his way to the front door to lock it before heading through the room to the back of the cabin. He stopped dead in his tracks as he entered the kitchen. "Did I-" he started, pausing in disbelief at the sight of his back door sitting wide open.

Looking around the dark kitchen, he saw a shadow in the corner opposite the door.

Leaving The Bonfire

IT WAS ONE OF those nights in the mountains where every star shone down like a spotlight on the earth. Justin sat on a fallen log, lost in thought as he stared at their reflection in the pond. A cool evening breeze caused him to shiver, pulling him out of his trance. He looked around at his friends, still partying around the bonfire before looking at his watch. He had originally planned on being home by now, but after getting caught up in his thoughts and emotions, he had completely lost track of time.

He walked over to Billy, who was standing about ten feet away, talking to some friends with a beer in his hand. As he approached and caught Billy's attention, he looked at his watch again, "We need to get moving. I wanted to be home by now."

Billy nodded. "Where's Kevin?" he asked.

Justin looked around and deflated as he spotted Kevin, passed out in the grass by the tree line. "He's over there. Passed out," he said, rolling his eyes.

"Every fucking time, man. I swear," Billy said, clearly frustrated.

They grabbed a few friends to help them carry Kevin to Justin's truck. Getting him in the back seat was far from an easy task.

"Why not just put him up front?" one of the men helping had asked.

"I'm not squeezing in that tiny back seat because his drunk ass passed out," Billy replied in anger.

They finally managed to get Kevin into the back seat, accidentally slamming his head against the rear window as he did so.

"Whadaryou mudderfuckers doin a me?" Kevin managed to say, sounding as if his mouth was full of sand.

Everyone laughed at this before walking away and leaving Justin and Billy with their drunk friend.

"You better not puke in my truck, Kev," Justin said, pointing at Kevin, who had already began snoring.

"He does this every time. I don't know why you still bring him to these bonfires," Billy said, his frustration still showing.

"Now's not the time, Bill," Justin said, cutting the conversation off.

As he began the thirty-minute drive back to his cabin on Horse Mill Hollow, Justin once again found himself lost in thought. This had been happening to him a lot lately, as his life just wasn't leading in the path he'd hoped it would.

Here he was, in his mid-twenties, and already a recovering alcoholic stuck in a dead-end job. He'd once had a good job working for the gas company, but he lost it when he was caught drunk driving in the company vehicle. With the job market as shitty as it was in his county, the only work he could find was a clerk position at a local gas station.

With the pay cut he'd had to take after losing his job, he was forced to move into the hunting cabin his family owned at the end of Horse Mill Hollow; a long, one lane dirt road that traversed through the woods for a few miles, eventually hitting a fork that led to two hunting cabins. His father lived in the cabin at the end of the right fork, and Justin lived in the one to the left.

While his father loved the seclusion of living alone out in the woods, Justin had grown to hate it. Sure, it was peaceful at times, but he hated the long, rough drive back and forth to the main road, especially since it was a good fifteen to twenty minutes further to get to any semblance of civilization once you got to that road.

Along with all of that frustration, there was also dealing with the heartache of having to keep his relationship with Billy on the downlow. They had been friends for years, and secretly attracted to each other the whole time until one night, after one too many beers, both had let their inhibitions go. They woke up snuggled together in bed the next morning and had been in a secret relationship ever since.

Neither had wanted their friends, nor the people in town to know about it, for fear of being ostracized or worse. People in the rural areas often didn't take too well to those who didn't fit inside the small box they were familiar with.

They were a little more than halfway back to the cabin when Justin felt Billy's hand creep across the middle of the seat and grab his. He pulled his hand away and looked over to see Billy sitting there, a confused look on his face.

"What?" Billy asked.

"Did you have to avoid me all night?" Justin asked.

"I just don't want to be suspicious around people," Billy said, defensively.

"Dude, we've been friends for years. If anything, being standoffish would be more suspicious."

"I'm sorry," Billy began, remorse in his eyes, "I'm just scared is all. I don't want anyone to start shit."

"I don't either, but I also don't want to spend the night acting like strangers. I'd rather we just stay at my place instead."

"Dude," Billy said, nodding his head in Kevin's direction.

"He's passed out drunk, Billy. He may as well not even be here."

Kevin laughed, quietly, from the back seat, causing both Justin and Billy to look back.

"I already know about you two. I figured it out a while ago. Most of us did," Kevin said, his speech a little less slurred than it had been just before they left.

"Fuck," Justin said with a sigh.

"Nobody cares, bro," Kevin began, pausing to hiccup before continuing, "Most of those dudes love you like brothers. They're kinda weirded out about it, but if shit went down, they'd have your back."

"Really?" Justin asked.

"Yeah, so just hold his hand and stop being a little bitch. I'm trying to sleep back here."

Smiling, they both laughed at this. Feeling a bit more relaxed, Justin put his hand in Billy's, and they turned onto Horse Mill Hollow.

.

The Broadcast

THEY STARTED DOWN THE long dirt road. The mass of trees that shrouded the road in complete darkness made the path lit up by the headlights ahead almost look like a tunnel. It was almost serene until the song on the radio was cut off by the sound of an emergency alert siren. After the series of obnoxiously loud beeps, a robotic voice began speaking.

"The department of homeland security has issued an emergency alert for central West Virginia."

"Homeland security?" Billy asked.

Justin held his hand up, "Shhh".

"There have been multiple reports of strange noises and lights in thy sky from regions of Clay County, Roane County, Kanawha County, Braxton County, and Nicholas County."

"What the fuck," Justin muttered quietly.

"We advise everyone to stay inside until further information is gathered. If you are outside, get somewhere safe as soon as possible. Lock all doors and windows. If possible, barricade any possible entrance to your residence. If you see or hear something outside, do not engage with it. Stay safe, stay armed, and stay alert."

The obnoxious beeping began again. Once it was finished, the radio went silent.

"This has to be a joke or something," Billy said, feeling Justin squeezing his hand tighter, "Someone tapped into the radio station's signal or something."

"You think so?" Justin asked.

"Yeah. It's like that thing from the sixties. That radio play that had an entire town spooked. It was a book, I think."

"War of the Worlds," Justin answered.

"Yeah. That one. It has to be."

"Or that Max Headroom shit from a few years ago," Kevin chimed in from the back seat.

"The dude from the Coke commercial? What did he do?" Billy asked.

"It was in Chicago or something. Someone hijacked a TV station and had some weird shit with Max Headroom, only it wasn't the real Max Headroom," Kevin said, his slur slightly better, despite his head being down as if he was sleeping.

"I think I remember seeing that on the news. Shit was cre..." Justin stopped at the sound of cracking coming from outside the truck. He and Billy looked up to see a tree falling. It landed in front of them, blocking the road. They both sat there and stared in awe.

"What happened?" Kevin asked.

"A fucking tree just fell across the road," Justin replied.

"That sucks," Kevin said with a laugh.

"What are we gonna do?" Billy asked.

"Hold on," Justin said, opening the door and stepping out of the truck.

"What the fuck?" Billy whispered to himself as he watched Justin open the toolbox in the back of his truck.

There was the sound of metal clanging for a moment before Justin reappeared at the driver's side door with a chainsaw, "I helped a friend cut down a tree in his yard last weekend. Forgot to put this back in the shed."

"Awesome!" Billy exclaimed.

"There should be another pair of gloves back there somewhere," Justin began, pointing towards the bed of the truck, "Go ahead and grab them. I'll start cutting at the tree, and you can help me carry the pieces away."

Billy nodded and opened his door. Justin walked up to the fallen tree and started up the chainsaw. He managed to cut a few pieces of the trunk away before realizing that Billy hadn't come up to start helping him yet.

Shutting off the chainsaw, he turned to look back at the truck. He couldn't see much of anything past the blinding headlights.

"Billy!" he called out, "You coming?"

He waited a moment for a response, but it never came. "It's cool. I'll just get it myself," he muttered as he set the chainsaw down and began pushing the pieces he had cut from the tree out of the road.

Once finished, he began to grow concerned. Making his way back to the truck, he called out once more, "Couldn't find the gloves back there?"

Still, there was no answer. As he approached the truck, he made a circle around it. He didn't see Billy anywhere.

Popping his head in the truck, he looked back at Kevin, "Where'd Billy go?" he asked.

"Huh?" Kevin asked, barely moving his head as he did so.

"Billy. He was supposed to grab gloves out of the back and help me, but he's gone."

"That's not cool," Kevin said.

Justin let out a loud sigh before turning around and cupping his hands around his mouth. "Billy!" he called out, moving around in a circle as he did so.

He froze at the sight of a dark silhouette in the dim red glow of the taillights. He wasn't sure what he was looking at, but he knew it wasn't Billy. The figure was very slim and crouched in a strange position.

He was just about to call out for Billy once more when the thing he was looking at stood from its crouched position. His heart raced as he stared ahead at the abnormally tall figure. Just then, it began moving toward him.

"Oh, fuck!" he called out as he turned and jumped into the truck.

He quickly threw the truck into gear and pressed the pedal to the floor. The tires spun out for a few seconds in the mud before finally gaining traction and moving forward.

The truck flew through the path Justin had carved out into the fallen tree, bouncing as it made its way along the rough dirt road. In the rearview mirror, he could see Kevin bouncing around in the back seat.

Grabbing the seat with one hand and pushing against the roof of the truck with the other, Kevin called out, "What the fuck, man?"

"There's something back there," Justin said, his voice shaking as he hit bumps in the road.

"Where's Billy?" Kevin asked.

"I don't know. I was looking for him but saw something off in the distance. Thing was like ten feet tall. I wasn't sticking around to see what it was."

In that moment, it was as if Kevin completely sobered up. The emergency broadcast, along with the fear in Justin's voice snapped him into reality. "Is it following us?"

"I don't know. It started moving towards us and I took off."

The cabin was just up ahead. Justin kept the truck's speed where it was, slamming the brakes and stopping it a mere four feet from the porch steps. Within seconds, both he and Kevin were out of the truck and entering the cabin.

"Help me lock the doors and windows!" Justin said as he began making his way around the cabin.

They locked every door and window before each grabbing a rifle from the gun cabinet and shutting off the lights. They crouched down at one of the front windows and peeked through the curtains to see if, whatever Justin had seen, followed them back to the cabin.

At such a close proximity, Justin felt Kevin's arm brush against him multiple times. Looking over, he saw Kevin scratching his neck.

"Fucking mosquitos on that pond, man," Kevin said.

"You..." Justin began, "you think Billy's okay?"

"I don't know, man. I hope so," he paused for a moment, before adding, "Whatever happens, I want you to know I meant what I said earlier. I won't say anything to anybody if you don't want me to, but what I told you is true. Some of us have talked about it before, and nobody would give you guys shit, man."

Justin started to respond but stopped at the sound of a helicopter in the distance. Both he and Kevin about had their faces glued to the window, staring intently to see what was happening.

As the helicopter got closer, they saw a spotlight shining down into the trees. In a flash, as it moved across the clearing, they caught sight of the creature Justin had seen earlier standing there. They both jumped back and gasped at this.

The spotlight quickly moved back onto the creature and froze. Gunfire erupted from above. The creature let out an ear-piercing shriek as some of the shots hit it and brought it to the ground.

"Holy fuck!" Justin called out, "Is it dead?"

The spotlight lingered on the creature for a few more seconds before moving on, as if looking for another target.

After a moment of silence, Billy finally spoke up, "I think so. I mean, it didn't move. That's probably why they flew off, to look for another one."

"I need to know," Justin began, "so I can look for Billy."

"You sure, man?" Kevin asked as Justin stood up and walked over to the gun cabinet.

"Yeah, I'm sure," he said, pulling two flashlights from the cabinet, "You can stay here if you want, but I'm going out to check."

"I'm not letting you go alone, dude. Give me one of those flashlights," Kevin said, holding his hand out.

Justin nodded and handed it to him. They slowly made their way to the door. Opening it, Justin stepped out and looked around. He could see the silhouette of the thing still lying on the ground.

Stepping off the porch, he turned on the flashlight and walked towards the creature. Kevin turned on his light and followed.

They both cringed as they approached the creature. Its slimy gray skin looked as if it was coated in mucous. Its slender, emaciated body gave the appearance of a person who hadn't eaten in years.

As they moved their lights along the thing's body, they spotted small holes scattered throughout, most likely from the bullets. A dark, syrupy fluid dripped from each one. They half expected the head to be the stereotypical alien head they had seen in drawings, but instead, it was more like a misshapen human head.

There were two small holes in place of a nose, and a narrow slit where a mouth would be. Its eyes were large, like most depictions of aliens, but more rounded rather than the stereotypical teardrop shape.

While its body lay completely still, Justin noticed its eyes blinking.

"I think it's still alive," he said with a shaky voice, "look at its eyes."

It must have blinked again as soon as Kevin looked, because he immediately jumped back, "Fuck!"

Wasting no time, Justin pointed the barrel of the rifle at the thing's head. Before Kevin could say anything, the gun went off. They both stared on in horror as they watched the thing's head explode into pieces. Neither of them moved until a few minutes later, when the sound of approaching footsteps interrupted the silence.

Guns pointed in the direction of the sound, both Justin and Kevin stood at the ready, fingers on their triggers.

"Don't shoot! It's me!" a voice called out before a shadow came running out from the trees.

Lowering his gun, Justin stood in disbelief.

"Billy?" he called out.

Justin immediately dropped his gun and ran out towards Billy, embracing him in a hug as they met. Billy grabbed both sides of his face and pulled him in for a kiss before speaking, "I'm sorry. That thing came after me. I tried screaming, but you couldn't hear me over the chainsaw. I ran off into the woods to draw it away. It followed me for a while, but then it came back for you."

"I'm just glad you're okay," Justin said, still holding Billy tightly.

"Hey, uh, guys," Kevin called out, "I'm happy for y'all, but we should probably get back inside. There might be more of those things out here."

Realizing he was right; they ended their embrace and began running back to the cabin. They froze at the sight of lights coming from the sky over the woods. The lights lingered there, looking like stationary lightning bolts as they pulsed.

"What the fuck is that?" Justin asked.

"I saw that earlier too, but it was over there," Billy said, pointing to the left, "Whatever it is, it's moving."

Justin picked up his rifle from the ground and the three of them ran into the cabin, turning off their flashlights and locking the door behind them.

The Trouble With Kevin

THEY SAT ON THE floor of the living room, Justin and Billy beside each other, and Kevin just across from them. None of them knew what to say, so they just sat there in silence, hoping it would all be over soon.

Eventually, Kevin spoke up, breaking the silence, "Do you have a radio or anything we can listen to. You know, see if there are any updates?"

"Fuck. I didn't even think of that," Justin said, standing up and walking to another room.

He returned with a small transistor radio. Turning it on, he moved the tuner back and forth, but found only silence. He continued playing with it until he heard Billy speak up, "Dude. What's up with your neck?"

"Mosquito or something. It's been itching like crazy," Kevin responded.

"No. Not that. It's… it's glowing or something," Billy said, concern in his voice.

"What?" Justin said, turning around, "What the fuck?"

The spot that Kevin had been scratching on his neck was pulsing a glowing red light from beneath the skin. He sat there, a terrified look on his face, "What? What do you mean glowing?"

"Go look in the mirror, dude!" Billy exclaimed.

In a panic, Kevin stood up and ran to the bathroom. "Fuck! What the fuck, man!?" he called out.

Billy and Justin both ran to the bathroom to find him pacing back and forth.

"It's gotta be some kind of tracker or something. Must have gotten me while I was asleep."

"What does that mean?" Justin asked.

"Probably that more are coming. They know we're here. They've targeted us for some reason... and we just killed their friend."

"Oh fuck! Oh fuck," Kevin screamed in a panic. "Get it out, man. You have to get it out. We have to flush it or something."

Justin and Billy looked at each other, scared and unsure what to do.

"I'm fucking serious, man," Kevin screamed, "Get a knife or something. Cut this fucking thing out."

Justin turned and ran to the kitchen. Fumbling through drawers before returning with the skinning knife he used for field dressing deer and a flashlight. "Here, hold this," he said, turning on the flashlight and handing it to Billy before turning back to Kevin, "Lay your head there, on the ledge of the tub."

Kevin did as Justin said, his panic rising, "Come on, man. Hurry up!"

Billy held the flashlight steady on Kevin's neck. Justin knelt down beside him. Bringing the knife to Kevin's skin, he hesitated for a moment.

"Dude, I don't care if it hurts. Just cut it out."

Taking a deep breath, Justin held the blade against Kevin's skin, just below the red pulsing light. He sliced the skin fairly deeply, but careful not to go too deep.

After making the incision, he stuck his finger in the hole to feel around for the device.

With his teeth clenched, Kevin let out a groan that was clearly a scream being held back.

"I can feel it!" Justin screamed, "I think I've got it!"

Justin dug around some more before pulling his hand back and making another incision with the knife, this time, in the opposite direction, making a cross pattern. Kevin did his best to hold back screams from pain as Justin stuck his thumb and forefinger into the hole in an attempt to get the device.

"It's like, stuck or something. I can't get it out." He grabbed Billy and pulled him closer, "Hold the light right here," he said, positioning the light mere inches from the hole in Kevin's neck.

Sticking his thumb and forefinger back in, he pulled the skin on Kevin's neck apart to get a good look at the device. It looked like a small marble. It had a silver tone to it in the moments it wasn't emanating a red light from inside. At the base of the device, silver wires spiderwebbed out into Kevin's muscle tissue like a root system.

"Oh no," Justin said, a defeated tone in his voice.

"What? What is it?" Kevin asked. He was beginning to cry.

"It's embedded itself. It has like, roots or something."

"Can't you get it out?" Kevin asked.

"I'm afraid to cut any deeper. I'm not a doctor, but I know there's important shit in there. It could kill you."

"Goddamnit!" Kevin cried out.

They stood there in silence while Kevin remained on the floor crying. After a few moments, he looked up at them with pleading eyes, "Can you guys give me a minute?"

Justin and Billy both nodded and walked back to the living room to give him time to think.

"What are we going to do?" Justin asked in a whisper.

"I don't know, Jus. If we can't get that thing out, more of those things will probably end up coming here," Billy paused, looking back and forth at the windows in the room, "Hell, for all we know, they're already here."

His statement sent a chill down Justin's spine.

"We," Billy began, "we could just-"

"No," Justin interrupted, "we're not going to leave him here alone."

Billy put his head down and nodded, "You're right. I'm sorry. I'm just scared."

"Me too, Billy. Me too."

Billy pulled Justin into his arms and held him tightly. They could feel each other's heart racing in fear. They stayed like that until Kevin called out to them.

"Justin. Can you come here for a minute?"

Justin pulled away, nodding at Billy before making his way to the bathroom.

"I figured out what we need to do," Kevin said as Justin entered.

"What do you mean?"

"Do you have your keys?" he asked.

"Yeah," Justin replied, "Why?"

"Let me see them," Kevin said, holding his hand out.

Justin pulled the keys from his pocket and handed them to Kevin. Before he could ask why he wanted them, Kevin grabbed him by his hair and shirt. With a pull, he moved to the side and threw Justin into the bathtub. As soon as he let go, he ran out of the bathroom door and shut it, wedging something underneath it. Justin was already banging on the door, trying to open it by the time Kevin made it back out to the living room.

Billy turned to Kevin and opened his mouth to speak, but before he got a single word out, Kevin had grabbed a lamp from an end table and smashed it against the side of his head.

As Billy crouched down in pain, Kevin ran for the front door. As he stepped out, he looked back to Billy, who was holding his head, blood running between his fingers, "Take care of each other. Hopefully, I'll see you on the other side."

"Wait! No!" Billy said, standing up.

"Come get me, fuckers!" Kevin screamed as he ran to the truck.

Billy ran after him, but the truck had already taken off by the time he got to the bottom of the porch steps. He fell to his knees and deflated at the sight of Kevin driving off down the road at a high speed.

Justin managed to get the bathroom door open and ran outside to find Billy on his knees, crying.

"That crazy fucker," he said, shaking his head.

They could hear screeching off in the trees. Looking at each other in fear, they quickly ran back into the cabin and locked the door.

The Morning After
(Billy)

WE STAYED UP FOR a while, holding each other while sitting in silence after Kevin took off with the truck. It wasn't until sunrise that we even bothered moving from the couch. We knew we weren't in the clear yet, but something about the sun being out made us feel a little safer.

As we stood from the couch, our intention was to head to bed to get some sleep, but we got distracted along the way. Chalk it up to the events of the night or Kevin's revelation about our friends and our relationship status, but we made passionate love before falling asleep. It was a much-needed distraction from the chaos of the evening.

The next morning, I woke up before Justin. For a while, I just lay there, watching him sleeping peacefully. I began to zone out, and memories from the night before played over in my head.

———◆———

Stepping out of the truck, I watched Justin head towards the tree with the chainsaw. I walked to the back of the truck to the open toolbox and dug around, looking for gloves. When I finally found them, I slipped them on and turned to find that... thing standing right in front of me.

My heart felt as though it would beat out of my chest. Every muscle in my body tensed up. I'm surprised I didn't piss myself.

Raising its hand, the thing extended its elongated looking finger and touched my forehead. Visions flooded my mind; dozens of images, giving me some answers as to what was going on as they flashed by in a micro-second.

I must have blacked out after that, because the next thing I knew, I found myself crouched behind a tree, hugging my knees to my chest. My eyes were closed, and I was rocking back and forth.

Somehow, I managed to find the dirt road again, and began making my way back to Justin's cabin. I spent that entire walk praying that I would make it there safely and that Justin was still okay.

Justin snored and rolled over, snapping me out of the memory trance I had fallen into. My heart sank a little, feeling guilty for not telling Justin what had really happened out there, not revealing what the thing had shown me.

I knew I had to tell him at some point, but I couldn't just yet, not while he still had a fighting spirit. I knew that if what I saw was true, and he knew about it, that spirit would die off quickly. I had to keep that spirit alive in him and hopefully harness some of it for myself. I had to hope that what I had seen was just a potential outcome, and not a set-in-stone vision of what was to come.

Making sure not to wake him, I slowly slid off the bed and stood up. I looked out the window, seeing what looked like a beautiful fall day outside before making my way to the bathroom.

After throwing some water on my face, I stood at the sink, looking back and forth from the mirror to the blood on the bathtub and floor. I thought about the tracking device we found in Kevin's neck. I wondered if I had one too.

Stepping back from the mirror, I began inspecting every inch of my body, using my reflection to inspect the parts I couldn't see on my own. After going over everything twice, I closed the door, turned off the light, and stuffed a bunched-up towel below the door to block out all light to check again; this time, keeping my eye out for any pulsating light.

The fact that I seemed free and clear of any tracking device did little to ease my nerves. That thing touched my head, and who knows what happened during the time that I blacked out. For all I knew, it could just have a tracker implanted deeper than the one inside

Kevin. That thing may have done a better job concealing it with me.

I could hear Justin stirring just outside of the bathroom, so I put the towel back up and stepped out into the hall, playing it off as if I had just been using the toilet. I looked into the bedroom to find Justin sitting on the end of the bed, a groggy look in his eyes.

"There you are," he said with a half-smile. "How long you been up?"

"Just a few minutes. I'll go grab us something to eat, then we can try to figure..." I trailed off, pausing to think of what to say, "something out."

Justin nodded solemnly and stood up. As he made his way to the bathroom, I headed into the kitchen. I cracked a few eggs and cooked them up on a skillet, thankful that the power was still on. It was probably only a matter of time before that changed.

Justin sat down at the table just as I was finishing. He didn't say a word until I set his plate in front of him.

"I want to go check on my dad," he said, "I need to see if he's okay."

"You think it's safe out there?" I asked.

"I don't know. Probably not, but I can't just leave him out there. If he's okay, we should all be together."

I nodded.

"You don't have to go if you don't want."

I dropped my fork, feeling offended, "You really think I would make you do that by yourself? Of course I'll go with you. Last night was scary enough. I'm not leaving your side again."

He gave me a look of recognition before nodding. For a moment, I saw a bit of the fear he experienced last night resurface. He was clearly just as worried as I was while we were apart.

Frank's Cabin
(Billy)

WE FORMED A PLAN as we finished breakfast. After getting a shower and getting dressed, we began putting our plan to action.

Stepping outside, we checked to make sure we didn't see anything before heading to the shed to get Justin's four-wheeler ready. Pushing the four-wheeler outside, Justin went back in and grabbed the gas can to begin filling up the tank. While he did that, I grabbed everything from the shed that could be used as a weapon and carried it to the cabin. Having positioned himself so I wouldn't leave his line of sight, Justin watched as I carried a pickaxe, a shovel, an ax, a pitchfork, and a hoe to the cabin and set them just inside the door.

After finishing up with all of that, we each grabbed a rifle from the cabin, locking the door behind us before hopping on the four-wheeler.

"You think the engine will attract those things?" I asked.

"I don't know, but we don't have much choice. Walking would take forever, and there ain't much daylight left."

I nodded. "Let 'er rip."

Turning the key, the engine came to life, and we made our way down the dirt road toward the fork. I kept lookout while Justin drove, hoping to not see anything emerge from the woods.

As we got to the fork, Justin paused before heading in the direction of his dad's cabin. We both looked off into the distance, our gaze lingering on the fallen tree he had cut through the night before. I couldn't tell if the shudder I felt was me, him, or a combined emotion.

Shaking his head, Justin turned the handle and began making his way towards the cabin. We pulled up a few minutes later to find his dad's truck sitting out front and the front door wide open.

Bringing the four-wheeler to a stop just behind the truck, Justin killed the engine. "Dad! You in there?" he called out.

We sat there for a moment, hoping to hear a response.

"Fuck," Justin said, "let's head inside."

It had been a while since I'd been in his dad's cabin, and I had forgotten how badly it reeked of cigarettes.

"Goddamn," I said, waving my hand in front of my face, "even with the door open this place smells like an ashtray."

"Yeah," Justin began, "his smoking has steadily gotten worse since he's lived on his own. Probably nothing else to do."

We made our way around the cabin, checking every room; even checking the bedroom closet and kitchen pantry. There was no sign of him. I stepped up to the back door, which was also sitting wide open, and called out, "Frank!"

With no response, I turned to find Justin beginning to pace back and forth between the kitchen and living room. "This isn't good, Billy. This isn't good at all. His boots are still by the door, his cigarettes and lighter are still on the table," he paused, picking up the beer can that sat on the table, "hell, he didn't even finish his beer. It's like he just vanished."

I headed into the living room. I looked around as Justin plopped himself on the couch. "The TV is still on too," he said, gesturing towards the TV that looked to be as old as we were.

With my attention directed toward the TV, I noticed the VHS tape sticking out of the VCR. Walking over toward it, I pulled it out. "Busty Beach Bimbos," I read aloud, "guess he rubbed one out before he left. Probably where you're sitting right now," I said with a laugh, pointing to where Justin was sitting.

He gave me a disgusted look as he jumped up from the seat. "Fucking gross, Bill."

"What?" I responded, attempting to lighten the mood some, "he's not a bad looking guy for his age."

"He's my dad, Bill. It's gross."

"I'm just saying. You take after him more than your mom. I wouldn't mind if you looked like him when you got older."

"Thanks, I guess," Justin said, lightening up a little.

"Sorry. What should we do though? Check the woods?" I asked.

"No," Justin replied, "No time for that. Let's just... leave a note or something, in case he comes back. Tell him to meet us at the cabin."

"Think we should grab some food and stuff before we go? We don't know how long we'll be holed up in that cabin for."

"Yeah. Probably a good idea," Justin said, walking back to the kitchen. "We'll leave some for him in case he comes back. Load the rest in the bed of the truck. I'll drive it back and you can follow me in the four-wheeler."

"How will he get to your cabin if we take his truck?" I asked.

"He has a four-wheeler too. I'll put that in the note."

I nodded.

Justin's dad wasn't one to stock up or be prepared for things, so there wasn't much there. We both shook our heads at the little bit of water and non-perishable food we could find before getting started carrying it to the truck.

"What would he do if there was a blizzard or something," I asked.

"Probably just starve until he could get out to get more food. That, or he would show up at my door," he replied with a laugh.

After carrying the last of what we planned to bring, I paused, looking at the liquor bottles on the kitchen counter.

"Fuck it," Justin said, pointing toward the bottles, "grab them too. The stubborn asshole is more likely to come to my cabin if he knows we have the booze."

I nodded and grabbed them. Justin sat down at the kitchen table and began writing his note while I carried them out to the truck. After setting the bottles in the truck, I read the note before heading back outside.

Dad,

Came looking for you. Some crazy shit going down. We grabbed a few things and took your truck. If you find this note, grab your four-wheeler and meet me at the other cabin. If you don't already know what's going on, I'll fill you in as best I can when you get here.

Justin

P.S. We took your booze too. Get your ass over here.

I knew Justin was worried about his dad, but I was glad to see he could still have a sense of humor in a time like this. I hoped, for his sake, that his dad was okay, and that we would see him soon. In my gut, though, I knew something bad had happened to Frank. Like Justin had said, he was a stubborn man. Whatever went down here last night, I knew he didn't just hide inside. That man didn't take shit from anyone. I just hoped that, if he did die, he at least went down fighting.

I heard the truck start up outside, so I ran out the door and hopped on the four-wheeler. Getting it started, I looked up at the truck, making eye contact with Justin through the side mirror. He nodded in acknowledgement, and we headed back to the cabin.

Back To The Bonfire

The Night Before

The party at the bonfire was going very well. More people than expected showed up. It made Cliff happy to see this many of his friends together at one time, in particular, the ones he didn't get to see very often.

He organized these bonfire parties at the pond on the edge of his property a few times a year, but this was the first time he had seen Justin and Billy at one in quite a while. As of late, Justin was usually unable to come because he was stuck working at the shitty gas station on the edge of town, and Billy rarely showed up to anything if Justin couldn't make it.

Growing up on the same street, Cliff and Justin had been good friends for about as long as they could remember. As a result of this, they had always remained pretty close.

Cliff had heard the rumors circulating around their large group of friends about Justin and Billy being a couple. He didn't pick up on it at first, but once the idea was planted in his head, he had no doubt it was true. He'd always felt something about Justin was different, but he couldn't pinpoint what it was.

Deep down, he didn't care if they were a couple. He loved Justin like a brother and respected him, and Billy seemed like a pretty good guy as well. On the rare occasion he overheard anyone shit talking their potential relationship, he would quickly shut it down.

He found himself concerned for the two of them as the party went on, noticing the distance that seemed to be between them. He'd barely seen them around each other all night, and Justin carried on as if something was bothering him. He was just about to make his way over to ask if he was okay when he saw them talking, looking around for Kevin, the friend they had brought with them.

He watched on as someone pointed over toward the tree line, quickly noticing Kevin passed out in the grass. With a laugh, he headed in that direction, figuring they would need help getting him up.

"Everything okay, guys?" Cliff asked as he approached Justin and Billy.

"It'll be better once we get his drunk ass in my truck. I need to get home," Justin said.

Cliff assisted in carrying their drunk friend to the truck and the struggle to get him in the back seat, laughing when Kevin's head slammed against the back window. He slurred something when this happened, though Cliff couldn't make out the words.

With Kevin loaded up in the truck, Billy hopped in the passenger seat and closed the door. Cliff stopped Justin on his way to the driver's side.

"You good, man?" he asked.

"Yeah," Justin answered, a concerned look on his face. "Why? What's up?"

"Just making sure, man. Haven't heard from you in a while." Justin nodded before Cliff continued, "Call me once in a while. Okay? I miss you, buddy."

Justin smiled at this and nodded, "I will."

Cliff waved before heading back towards the bonfire. He grabbed a drink and began socializing some more, watching some of his friends slowly disperse here and there.

A while later, he headed over to the cooler to grab what would be his last beer for the night when he heard a few people gasp.

"What the fuck is that?" one of them called out.

Turning to see what was wrong, Cliff dropped the can of beer to the ground and stood there in shock, his mouth hanging wide open.

Strange bolts of pulsating lights came down from the sky, lighting everything up more than the light of a full moon.

"It's just lightning," a drunken voice called out.

"Lightning strikes, it doesn't linger, dipshit," another said.

"Well, what is it, then?" the drunken voice said.

"Fuck if I know," someone said in reply, "Cliff, you seeing this shit?"

Unable to speak, Cliff joined his group of friends and nodded.

A few of the remaining people at the bonfire quickly ran back to their vehicles and left, presumably in fear. Cliff couldn't blame them. He had the urge to run back to his house and lock the doors himself.

He very quickly wished he had listened to this urge when he lights stopped and he noticed the silhouette of something standing among the trees.

"What is that?" a voice called out.

"What is what?" another replied.

"There," Cliff answered, holding out his shaking hand and pointing toward the trees. "In the trees. There's something there."

The drunken voice, which Cliff now registered as his friend Sam Spencer, spoke up again, "Whatever it is, it don't belong here."

Before anyone could respond, Sam pulled a revolver from his belt and ran towards the thing. As he got closer, he began shooting at it.

"Sam! You dumb fuck! Get back here!" Cliff called out, but Sam didn't listen. As he approached the tree line, the creature seemed to have disappeared.

"Where'd you go, you sonofabitch?" he called out.

"Get away from the trees, Sam!" Cliff screamed.

Sam turned to look back at Cliff and the few remaining partygoers. They all screamed as an elongated arm reached out from behind a tree and grabbed Sam by the head. He began flailing around and screaming. He fired his gun a few more times, expelling the last few bullets. After the last shot, they could faintly hear the clicking of the hammer against the empty chambers of the revolver.

Everyone ran back to their vehicles, peeling out and taking off towards the main road while Cliff stood there in shock, watching his drunken friend get lifted off the ground by his head.

The creature whipped its long arm to the side, slamming Sam's body against a tree as if it weighed nothing. Cliff could hear Sam screaming out in pain as he lay on the ground.

When the creature reached down to grab Sam once more, Cliff took advantage of the distraction and ran back to his house on the other side of the property. Without even looking back, he bolted for the door and opened it. Sam's screaming had stopped just before he made it inside.

He locked the doors before going around the house and repeating the action with every door and window before retreating to the basement. Grabbing a rifle, he shrunk down in the corner and pointed the barrel towards the door at the top of the stairs, just waiting for the creature to get inside.

Cliff's Journey

HAVING FALLEN ASLEEP AWAITING the creature's intrusion, Cliff woke the next day to silence outside and sunshine beaming through the windows.

Standing up, he stretched his tight muscles, hearing multiple joints crack and pop as he did so. *That cold floor was not a good place to doze off,* he thought to himself.

Making his way around the basement, Cliff peered through the small windows, checking to see if that thing from last night was still around. His heart sank at the sight of Sam's body on the ground off in the distance.

"Rest in peace, you crazy bastard," he said to no one before making his way upstairs.

After leaving the basement, he made his way through every room of the house, ensuring the coast was clear before letting his guard down some. He was surprised to see that none of the doors or windows seemed to have been tampered with.

Is it over? He wondered. *Is that thing gone? Are there more?*

He picked up the phone in an attempt to call someone, but the line was dead. He then headed to his living room and turned on the TV. While the cable networks were still live, the local ones were all down. Nothing but static on each one.

"Fuck!" he called out in frustration.

He grabbed something to eat from his pantry and waited around, trying anything to distract himself. After a few hours, he was going stir crazy. He wanted answers. He wanted to not be alone right now.

Giving up on waiting things out, Cliff grabbed a duffel from his closet and began packing some clothes and supplies in it. With that slung over his right shoulder and a rifle slung over his left, he grabbed his keys and headed outside to his truck.

As he made his way down the winding road that led to Horse Mill Hollow, he occasionally saw signs of more destruction from last night. Crashed vehicles here and there, even a few bodies, which he assumed were dead, but didn't stop to make sure.

Shortly before reaching the turn off for Horse Mill Hollow, he spotted Justin's truck, its front end smashed into a tree on the side of the road. He pulled over just beside the truck and got out to inspect it. The blood on the seat, along with bloody handprints on the driver's side made his heart sink.

Looking around, he called out, "Justin! Billy!"

He listened for a moment, but there was no response. He tried once more, and after a few minutes of waiting, gave up and got back in his truck.

Worried for his friend, he drove another mile or so down the road before turning onto Horse Mill Hollow. He slowly made his way down the rough dirt road, scanning his surroundings the entire time. He stopped at a fallen tree that had recently been cut through and gasped at the sight of a body lying on the ground just a few feet away. He could tell by the gray hair that it wasn't Justin, Billy, or Kevin, so he hopped in the truck and continued down the road.

Arriving at the fork in the hollow, he sat for a moment, trying to remember which cabin Justin was living in. He had been to both before back when they were younger but couldn't recall Justin telling him which one he had moved into.

Frustrated, and feeling like a child, he pointed to the one and began the famous rhyme, "Eeny, meeny, miny, moe, Catch a tiger by the toe. If he hollers, let him go, Eeny, meeny, miny, moe," stopping on the fork to the left.

With a sigh, he let off the brake and began driving down the left side of the fork. Before long, he pulled up to the cabin to find Justin and Billy talking on the porch.

Finding Frank
(Justin)

BILLY AND I HAD just finished carrying the last of dad's things into the cabin when we heard something approaching. We gave each other a knowing look before grabbing our rifles and pointing them in the direction of the sound.

As the vehicle came into view, I recognized it.

"That's Cliff," I said, lowering my gun. I looked over to see Billy still holding his rifle at the ready. "Dude, it's Cliff. Put the gun down."

"I'll put it down when I know for sure it's him," Billy said.

He wasn't wrong for being cautious, so I nodded and stepped off the porch, approaching the truck as it pulled in while making sure to stay out of the potential line of fire.

Cliff opened his driver's side window and began waving his hand as he pulled up to the cabin, presumably signaling Billy that he was a friend. As he stepped out, Billy lowered his gun.

"You guys are okay. Thank god," Cliff said as he walked towards us, a look of relief on his face. "I was worried when I saw your truck up the road."

"You saw it?" I asked, "Was Kevin there?"

"No," he answered, pausing, "Kevin had your truck?"

"Long story," Billy said, stepping off the porch to shake Cliff's hand, "Good to see you again. Glad you're okay too."

We invited Cliff inside. He grabbed his duffel from the truck before coming onto the porch and stepping inside. Closing the door behind him, he took a seat on the couch. I went into the kitchen and grabbed a bottle of bourbon from my dad's stash. I poured us each a shot and joined the two of them at the couch.

We each took our shot and began catching up on things. I started, filling Cliff in on what had happened with the tree, and with Kevin, answering his question as to why Kevin had my truck.

Cliff went on to tell us about what happened at the bonfire after we had left. I didn't really like Sam but was sad to hear about what happened to him.

Cliff then went on to tell us about his drive here; the things he saw along the way. I held up my hand and stopped him when he mentioned the body.

"Wait. A body? On this road? Where?" I asked.

"Right by the fallen tree," Cliff answered, "Just before it. Barefoot. Gray hair. I knew it wasn't you guys, so I kept going."

Billy gave me a knowing look as I stood up, "Dad! It was probably my dad. I need to go out there!"

"I'm sorry if it was your dad, but I'm pretty sure he was dead."

"How sure?" I asked.

"Like... ninety percent sure," Cliff added.

"That's not enough. I need to go check," I said, heading to the door.

Without saying a word, Billy and Cliff stood up, following me as I headed out the door. I had the truck started before they even got inside and took off as soon as the door closed.

I sped up the road, the truck bouncing as it traversed the dips and bumps along the way. I hit the brakes as soon as we made it past the tree. Looking to my left, I saw my dad's body laying there.

"I knew we should have checked here earlier," I said, shifting the truck to park. "I had a gut feeling."

Opening the door, I hopped out and ran over towards my dad. I knelt down beside him and began checking for signs of life. I could see his chest moving up and down, just slightly. Putting my hand to his neck, I felt a pulse. I looked up to see Billy and Cliff looking at me with sad eyes.

"He's alive. Help me get him to the truck!" I yelled, waving them over.

They ran over quickly and joined me at his side.

"Dude, I'm sorry," Cliff began.

"It's fine," I said, waving him off. "There's a lot of weird shit going on right now. I'm not mad. Just help me get him to the truck.

Billy took one arm while Cliff took the other. I grabbed both legs and together we lifted him off the ground and began carrying him to the truck. With three of us there, we opted to lay him in the bed of the truck to make things easier. As Billy jumped back to the ground, Cliff stayed on the bed.

"I'll stay back here with him."

I nodded and headed back to the driver's side. While I wanted to rush, I took it slow down the road, doing my best to keep my dad's limp body from bouncing around too much.

The sun was almost completely set by the time we got back to the cabin and carried my dad inside. With him still unconscious, we lay him on the couch.

Taking a step back, I looked down at him before turning back to Billy and Cliff, "I don't know what else to do right now."

They could hear the pleading tone in my voice. Billy gave me a sympathetic look as he approached me and pulled me in for a hug.

"I'm sure he's okay, Justin. Hopefully he'll wake up soon and we can figure something out."

I returned his hug. Glancing over at Cliff, I spotted a knowing look on his face, telling me that our hug confirmed his suspicions.

Without a word, he approached the two of us and patted us on the shoulder, giving a nod before heading into the kitchen.

As Billy pulled away from our hug, he looked directly in the eyes. "This gives me hope," he said.

I nodded.

"Not just for him. We need to talk."

I gave him a confused look as he grabbed the bottle of bourbon and headed into the kitchen, gesturing for me to follow.

"You too," I heard him say to Cliff, "have a seat."

I stepped in and joined him, wondering what he had to say. Wondering if it had anything to do with his brief disappearance the night before.

Secrets
(Billy)

HOLDING ONTO MY SECRET was killing me inside, especially now after finding Justin's dad, knowing he was alive. I couldn't keep what I knew, what I had seen, from Justin any longer. I had to let it out, so that's exactly what I did.

Once I had Justin and Cliff seated at the table, I took a swig from the bottle of bourbon and handed it to Justin. "Go on, you'll need it," I said.

He took the bottle from my hand and brought it to his mouth for a large swig before passing it to Cliff, who did the same.

"I've been going on all day wondering when and how to say this, but I need to just get it out."

Justin and Cliff stared on, curiosity and fear in their eyes.

"I'll start by saying what happened to me after we found that fallen tree," I paused before continuing.

"I went back to the toolbox to get the gloves you mentioned so I could help you move the tree as you cut it. Once I grabbed them, I turned to find that thing staring right at me. It reached out towards me, extending its finger, and touched me on the forehead. I saw visions, images, of what was going on. It played out like a long time had passed, but in reality, it was a second at most. The next thing I knew, I woke up crouched behind a tree. It took me a little bit, but I found my way back to the road... found my way back to you."

Tears began forming in my eyes at this, and I took a moment to breathe.

"What did you see? Do you remember any of it?" Justin asked, putting his hand on mine.

I nodded.

"For one, they're not aliens. At least not in the sense that we usually use that word."

"What do you mean?" Cliff asked.

"They're not from this world. They're from somewhere else; another dimension. Somebody... somewhere... opened a portal or something. That's what it looked like to me, anyway."

"Fuck," Justin said, barely audible.

"I don't know how, but someone did it. That's what caused the lights in the sky. It was a side effect of having a rift between two worlds. The thing we killed last night, it wasn't the only one, but Cliff's story already proved that to you."

"It just," Justin paused, "told you all of this?"

"Not exactly. It was like it fed the knowledge to me when it touched me, but I also saw some of it. I also saw tidbits of the aftermath. Death and destruction everywhere. Here in West Virginia first, then spreading out to the rest of the country and eventually, the world."

I broke down at this, remembering the horrifying images I saw.

"There was so much death. So much. Women, men, children, animals. Entire cities laid to ruin."

"So, we're doomed, then," Justin said, dejected.

I squeezed his hand a little tighter.

"Maybe not. You see, two of the things it showed me have already been proven lies. It showed me Cliff and everyone else from the bonfire, dead and lined up around the perimeter of the pond. It also showed me your dad, hanging from a tree."

They looked at me with concerned looks.

"If those visions were a lie, then maybe more of them are too. Maybe something beats these things or sends them back. Maybe we get out of this alive. Not just us, but humanity in general. You remember that helicopter last night? The one that shot that thing down before you blew its head off?"

Justin nodded.

"That wasn't in the vision it showed me. I think," I paused, "I think maybe it lied to me, like it was trying to make me lose hope. Maybe it hoped that despair would spread to you, and any others we may encounter, like a virus. If we lose hope, we're easier to defeat."

"That... actually makes sense," Cliff said, "the best way to take down an enemy is from the inside. It's a common strategy."

"So, what do we do, then?" Justin asked.

"I don't know. Maybe, for now, we just wait. Maybe that helicopter was the first of many to come. The military could be out there picking these things off one by one as we speak. I think we just give it time and see what happens. We have enough supplies here to last at least a week, and we have enough weapons to stave off any of these things if they come back as long as they don't ambush us."

"What about Kevin?" Justin asked. "That tracker thing, or whatever was in his neck. Did you get one too? We could be sitting ducks."

"I don't think so. I mean, I checked myself all over this morning. Multiple times. You can check me too if you want. Just to be sure."

I stood and began unbuttoning my shirt.

"Wait," Justin started, "You don't have to-"

"I want you to." I said, cutting him off. "Both of you. I've been freaking out about this all day. I checked, but I could have missed something. I need to be sure. I don't want to put either of you in danger."

Justin and Cliff both nodded, and I proceeded stripping down.

"Wait," Cliff called out as I grabbed the waistband of my underwear. "You... uh... don't have to," he paused and began blushing.

"It's not exactly a time for modesty, Cliff," I responded, breaking the silence.

"But you two..." he trailed off.

"Calm down, Cliff. It's not like I'm gonna suck his dick right in front of you," Justin said with a laugh.

Cliff chuckled for a moment before waving his hand dismissively, "Sorry. I'm an idiot. You're right."

I was grateful for Justin's joke, as it seemed to break the tension of the moment.

Continuing where I left off, I pulled off my underwear. They both surrounded me, each checking every square inch of my body for any bumps, cuts, or pulsing lights.

Once confident that I was fine, they both stepped away and I began putting my clothes back on. As I finished, I looked over at Cliff. "Your turn," I said.

"What?" he asked, confused.

"You saw me naked. I think it's only fair I get to see you naked now," I said with a wink.

"Asshole," Cliff said with a laugh. He stood up and began walking to the living room but froze dead in his tracks at the doorway. The look on his face was one of fear.

"What is it?" Justin and I asked in unison, approaching him.

"He's... he's up," Cliff said, pointing into the living room.

Not What He Seems
(Justin)

I STOOD UP AND walked to the doorway where Cliff was standing to see my dad standing there in front of the couch. He stood there with a blank expression on his face. His eyes looked lifeless, as though they were not focused on any specific thing.

"Dad?" I said, running over to him. I stood by his side and grabbed his arm. It rested limply in my grasp. The others quickly joined me, Cliff standing to his right side, and Billy just behind him.

I lifted my hand, snapping my fingers in his face, "Dad! Can you hear me? Are you okay?"

He quickly snapped to attention, looking straight ahead. The three of us jumped, startled by his sudden movement. His eyes looked like they were now focused on something, and he turned his attention to Cliff.

"It's me, Frank. It's Cliff," he said, his voice shaking.

Dad nodded his head slowly and pulled his arm from my grasp.

"What happened to you? Are you hur-"

I was cut off by dad reaching out and grabbing Cliff's face. Before any of us could react, he pulled Cliff in, as if for a kiss. Opening his mouth, he pulled Cliff's mouth to his.

Cliff began flailing and trying to scream. Billy grabbed Cliff from behind and I grabbed my dad. Together, we started pulling them apart. As their mouths pulled away from each other, I saw tendrils of something protruding from dad's mouth and into Cliff's. They looked like vines or tentacles, and they were moving in a swirling motion.

I looked to Billy, who had a frightened look on his face, and nodded.

Taking a deep breath, we pulled again, harder this time, and in a yanking motion. Whatever was coming from dad's mouth released Cliff, and they both fell backwards. I ended up on my back with my dad on top of me, and Billy ended up with Cliff landing just beside him.

I pushed dad off and sat up. Billy sat there in shock, and Cliff was on all fours, vomiting on the floor. Beside me, dad's body began twitching and letting out an ear-piercing shrieking sound.

Lifting off the floor, almost as if he was levitating, dad ended up back on his feet and began charging for Billy.

"No!" I screamed, standing up and running for the door. I bent down and grabbed the ax that lay on the floor just beside the door. I turned around to find dad with his hands gripping Billy's throat. His back was to me, and I could see Billy's face going red. I couldn't hear his choking gasps over the shrieking.

Through instinct, I lifted the ax and reared back. I hesitated for a moment. *Am I about to kill my dad?* I wondered.

"Kill it!" Cliff screamed, as if reading my mind. "Whatever that is, it's not your dad anymore."

"Fuck!" I screamed as I swung the ax.

It struck my dad in the neck, going about halfway through before stopping.

He let go of Billy and turned to face me, the ax still sticking out of his neck. With arms reached out, he began to charge towards me.

Thinking on his feet, Billy grabbed the ax, stopping my dad, and pulled. The ax came free from dad's neck, and he fell to the floor.

Not hesitating, Billy lifted the ax and swung, bringing it down on dad's neck a second time and almost completely severing it.

Dad, or more specifically, dad's body stood up, its head dangling from a small bit of tissue. The strange tendrils extended from his neck as if reaching for the head to pull it back in place.

As he began moving around, I reached out and grabbed his head by the hair. I yanked at it, pulling the small bit of tissue apart and freeing it from the rest of the body.

With tendrils flailing from its neck, the body began running around the room without direction, bumping into walls and furniture as it did so.

I looked to the gas fireplace, then to Billy, "Turn it on!" I screamed, pointing towards it.

Billy rushed over and turned on the gas before grabbing the box of matches that sat just beside it. With his hand shaking, he struggled to get the match lit. It was on his third try that he was successful, and he threw it into the fireplace. The gas ignited with a *poof* sound, and the fire burned at full force.

Once Billy moved out of the way, I tossed the head, which was still shrieking, into the fire.

Cliff tackled the body to the ground and held it there, doing his best to keep away from the protruding tendrils.

We watched as the head began to burn in the fire, filling the room with the putrid smell of burning hair and flesh.

"Guys, look!" Cliff shouted, drawing our attention to him.

The movement in dad's body and its tendrils began to slow down as the head burned. By the time most of the flesh and tissue had burned away and only the skull remained, the body had stopped moving completely.

"Billy!" I shouted, getting to my feet, "Grab the shovel." I turned to Cliff, "Grab the ax. Let's get him outside."

Knowing exactly what I had in mind, they did as I asked. Billy began digging two holes while Cliff and I got to work hacking dad's body into pieces. Once finished, we put the severed limbs in one hole, and the dismantled torso in the other. Cliff and I got on our hands and knees and began filling in one hole while Billy used the shovel to fill the other.

Exhausted, we made our way back into the cabin once finished. Cliff went straight for the bottle of bourbon that still sat on the kitchen table and took a big swig. I quickly joined him and took the bottle, taking a large swig myself before handing it off to Billy. He chuckled to himself after taking the shot.

"What's up?" I asked.

"Well, the fact that you two were inspecting my naked body just a bit ago doesn't seem quite as awkward now."

"Yeah," I replied, "having to dismember my possessed father really puts things in perspective."

We all laughed and took another swig before plopping down in our chairs around the table.

Drinks And Revelations
(Billy)

WE SAT AROUND THE table for a while, passing the bottle of bourbon back and forth, barely saying a word to each other. If I'm being honest, I don't think either of us knew what to say. All things considered, Justin seemed to be taking the loss of his dad pretty well, though I assumed that it would hit him once this was all over. If we made it out alive, that is.

At one point, I looked over to Cliff, holding out the bottle of bourbon to pass it to him, but he didn't look well.

"You okay, man?" I asked.

"No. Not really. I feel like shit. I think your dad, or whatever that was, did something to me."

I reached over to pat him on the shoulder, and it was as if a bolt of electricity went through me. Just like when that thing touched my forehead the night before, my head was flooded with visions.

I saw that thing reach into the truck after I had run away. It had something small in its hand, and it held it to Kevin's neck. *The tracker,* I thought.

I saw a bit more of how the portal was opened. A group of men standing around a large machine in a laboratory. I saw it powering up, then a large white glowing ball of energy expanded from it, killing the men as it did so.

The next vision was of tanks, helicopters, jeeps; men in uniforms with guns shooting down these things and the people they've infected. There were many shots, a lot of fire, and some explosions.

I could feel the fear these things were now feeling.

Oh shit, I thought, *we're winning!*

I could feel everything coming to a close soon. I knew in that moment that we just needed to wait this out a little longer.

When I came out of the vision, I jumped back in my chair, almost tipping it over. Justin was by my side immediately, concern all over his face.

"What happened? Are you okay?"

I looked at him with a smile. "We're gonna make it."

"What?" he asked.

"We're gonna make it!" I screamed, standing up from my chair, "We're gonna fucking make it!"

"What do you mean?" Cliff asked.

"I had another vision, as soon as I touched you. That helicopter we saw last night; there's so much more. Whatever those things are, we're beating them. Humanity is winning!"

Justin and Cliff sat there with wonder on their faces, listening as I told them all the details of the visions I'd had. I could see Justin's spirit rising as I told them. Cliff, on the other hand, wasn't quite as lifted.

"There's still one problem," Cliff said once I was finished. "What about me? What if I end up like," he paused, gesturing towards the living room, "him?"

"I'm sure you're fine, Cliff. We just need to wait it out," I said, attempting to reassure him.

"You guys have to kill me. You're good together, and you have each other to live for. I don't want to fuck that up by turning into some monster and killing you."

"Absolutely not!" Justin said. "We'll keep an eye on you. If it comes to it, we'll do it if we have to, but we're not just going to kill you for no reason."

"At least tie me up or something. Please. For your own safety."

I looked at Justin, "He does have a point."

He nodded before looking back to Cliff, "You sure?"

"Yeah. I'm sure."

Justin stood up and walked into another room while I sat there with Cliff. He returned shortly after rolling an old metal wheelchair into the room.

"Was my Pawpaw's. He used to come out here with us, even when he couldn't get around well," he said, answering my question before I could ask it.

"I remember," Cliff said as he stood up and made his way to the chair.

Once seated, we began tying him down. We tied his arms to the arm rests, his legs to the footrests, and his torso to the frame. We stood back as we finished, both feeling guilty for it.

"Y'all seriously need to stop. You won't feel bad if tentacles start coming out of my mouth," Cliff said, "one thing though."

"What's that?" I asked.

"I have to pee."

"Seriously?" Justin asked.

Cliff began laughing hysterically. We both rolled our eyes.

"Come on, man. I had to. The joke was right there."
"Ha ha," I said, mocking laughter.

"Oh Justin. If I had to pee, would you be kind enough to hold my dick for me, old friend?" he asked.

"You'd just get hard and ask me to jack you off, fucker," Justin replied.

"Wouldn't want to make ol' Billy boy here jealous. You'd never go back to him once you've had a piece of this."

"I've seen it," Justin said, "I wasn't impressed."

"What? When?" Cliff asked.

"We went to school together, dickbag. Gym class. Locker room."

"It's bigger now, though."

"I doubt it," Justin said.

We all laughed, appreciating levity after the events of the last two days. I followed Justin as he wheeled Cliff into the living room. He parked him by the TV and we both just about collapsed onto the couch.

We had just started to calm down when there was a knock at the door.

Visitor
(Billy)

"WHAT THE HELL?" I asked, looking at Justin, then at Cliff.

They both shrugged.

"Who is it?" Justin called out.

There was no answer. Only three more slow knocks. Spaced out just enough to chill all of us to the bone. Justin stood up and slowly crept over to the door.

"Wait," I whispered, holding up my hand.

I stood up and walked to the kitchen, grabbing the rifles we had leaned against the wall earlier. Keeping one in my hand, I handed the other over to him. He held it at the ready and I stepped in front of him to open the door.

Turning the knob slowly, I stepped back as I pulled the door open. I looked over to see Justin lower his rifle a few inches, a confused look on his face.

"What?" I whispered.

"There's nothing there," he whispered back.

He took a step forward, pausing before calling out again. "Hello?"

There was no response.

Slowly, Justin walked out the door. I looked out just in time to see something, or someone, tackle him. They tumbled down the steps to the ground. That's when the shrieking began again.

"Shit! Shit!" Cliff screamed as I ran outside to help Justin.

I looked down to see a man pinning Justin to the ground by his neck. I noticed the gash on the side of the man's neck, then noticed the clothing he was wearing.

It's Kevin!

I kicked my foot out, knocking Kevin off of Justin. He rolled to the side, and I shot him in the chest.

After my shot went off, Justin rolled to his belly and crawled across the ground to get out of the way.

The thing that used to be Kevin got back to its feet quickly. It turned its head back and forth as it continued shrieking, as if sending out a beacon to any of its buddies that might be close by.

"Shut the fuck up!" I screamed as I shot again, this time hitting it in the nose, causing the back of its head to blow out all over the ground behind it.

It stayed standing, still shrieking, only now, tendrils extended out of the entry and exit wounds left behind from the bullet.

I shot again, hitting it in the forehead this time. More pieces of bone and brain matter went flying, and the thing fell to the ground. I ran over and stomped on the remainder of its head to hold it there.

Justin returned, standing by my side with the ax. He began chopping at the thing, dismembering it piece by piece as I kept my foot pressed on its head. The tendrils began wrapping themselves around my boot and leg. Luckily, they hadn't gotten under my pants yet.

"Justin!" I called out, bringing his attention to my leg.

He quickly made work on the thing's neck, severing its head in two chops. As soon as it was detached, I tried pulling my leg back. The tendrils had a good grip on my boot and showed no signs of letting go.

"Hold still," Justin said as I began to panic.

Lifting the ax up, he brought it down on the thing's jaw, just below the sole of my boot. He held it there as I pulled. I fell to the ground and turned over to my belly, using my hands, along with my free leg to break free. As I pulled, I slowly felt them losing their grip. One more pull, and finally, I was free.

Justin lifted the ax, which was still stuck in the severed head. He slammed it to the ground, repeatedly, until it was reduced to mush.

With that taken care of, we looked over to the remainder of the body, which was flopping around on the ground in an attempt to get up.

Suddenly, Justin had a look on his face as if an idea had just struck him. Turning, he ran to the shed beside the cabin. He returned with the gas can from earlier and began dousing the body in gasoline.

While he did this, I ran inside to grab the box of matches from the fireplace. As I grabbed them, I happened to spot a pack of cigarettes on the ground, presumably from Justin's dad. I picked them up as well and ran back outside.

As if creating my own cheesy action movie ending, I pulled a cigarette from the pack and put it in my mouth. I struck a match on the side of the box and held it up to the cigarette to light it.

I took a deep drag from the cigarette before throwing the match onto the torso that lay on the ground by my feet. It ignited immediately, and quickly spread to the surrounding severed parts.

We stood there and watched the body burn until it stopped moving. Justin grabbed the cigarette from my mouth, taking a drag before throwing it to the ground.

"Smooth move, Rambo," he said, before turning to go back into the cabin.

I turned to follow him but stopped at the sound of engines approaching. We turned and looked back to see two military vehicles coming down the road. Men in uniforms stood in the back of each vehicle, guns at the ready. The sun was beginning to rise just behind them.

We walked out to them as they approached. And the men in the back hopped off to meet us.

"That one of the screamers?" the one asked, pointing the barrel of his rifle at the body burning in the yard.

"Yeah," I replied, "second one we've gotten tonight."

"Nicely done," the soldier said with a nod.

"What happens now?" I asked.

"You come with us to safety while our boys finish getting this situation contained."

"There's just one more thing," I said to the soldier.

"What's that?" he asked.

Justin and I both looked back at the cabin.

Epilogue
(Justin)

As LUCK WOULD HAVE it, what Billy had said earlier that night ended up being true. All we had to do was wait it out. The men loaded us up into one of their vehicles and Cliff into the other. They brought us to a facility in town that was much like the places FEMA sets up after natural disasters.

They kept everyone in these facilities with armed guards just outside as they finished what they called 'containing the situation.' What that really meant was they were killing off any remaining beings that had crossed over, along with the people that had been infected by them.

It was two weeks before they considered the area cleaned and deemed it safe to inhabit once more. Everyone returned to their homes to begin picking up the pieces of what was left of their life. From the stories I heard in that facility, Billy and I got off kind of easy.

The deaths in the area ended up opening up a lot of better jobs, which ended up helping me out tremendously. I was able to quit the gas station and got a job as an apprentice working on HVAC units.

I also ended up inheriting both cabins from my father once all the paperwork was cleared. I worked over the next few weeks getting both cabins cleaned up and sold them. I used the money to buy a place in town, where Billy and I live together. We no longer hide our relationship from anyone, and on the rare occasion some asshole decides to give us shit for it, we just make them sorry they said anything.

That's one good thing about fighting for your life against beings from another dimension; you no longer have any reservations about throwing hands at regular human beings.

Cliff ended up being quarantined for a while. He, along with a few other folks the soldiers came across had apparently been infected, but not enough to go full screamer like my dad and Kevin had. Nobody knew what they did or how they did it, but somehow, they eventually released Cliff, along with the others like him, and deemed them safe to be among the population.

Despite this, Cliff was never the same. He was still my friend and always would be, but there was something that had changed in him that went beyond emotional trauma. When they removed the infection from him, they took something else along with it.

It's been almost thirty years now. Billy and I are still doing well, and life seems good, but every so often, I look to the sky, and I look in the trees; just waiting to see those lights again. I don't know if I'll ever stop looking.

The End Of The Line
(Bonus Story)

JACK SAT AT THE table gritting his teeth as Phoebe, his Tinder date, rambled on about some mundane topic he couldn't care less about. Usually, he could deal with a woman who was somewhat annoying if it meant getting laid afterwards, but this woman was too much.

I'd rather fucking go home and jerk off, he thought to himself.

By the time they had finished their food, he was ready to pull his hair out. He sat there, wishing and hoping for a way out. To his surprise, it came just a few seconds later when Phoebe stood up and excused herself from the table.

"I'm gonna use the restroom real quick. Let's order a dessert to split when I get back," she said with a wink.

"Sounds good," Jack replied with a fake smile.

As soon as she was out of sight, he grabbed his jacket and headed for the door. Without looking back, he stepped outside and began running. He turned the corner into an alley a few blocks away, lighting a cigarette as he slowed his pace and walked the final few blocks to the nearest subway station.

With the station in sight, Jack threw his cigarette onto the ground and stepped on the escalator. He felt a chill run up his spine at how empty the station was. The hum of the escalator, which was usually barely noticeable, seemed deafening in the eerie silence. Even as he approached the bottom, he looked around and didn't see a single person waiting for the next train.

"Fucking creepy," he said out loud to himself.

To distract himself, Jack pulled his phone out of his pocket and unlocked the screen. He already had three missed calls and five text messages from Phoebe. Without responding, he cleared the notifications and went into her contact page to block her number. By the time he had finished, he heard the train approaching. He let out a sigh of relief, thankful that the wait in this creepy station hadn't been too long.

Just like the station, the train was also empty. He stood there, dumbfounded as he entered, not seeing a single person in any of the seats. With a shrug, he sat in the nearest seat and waited for the doors to close. To double check, he pulled out his phone again to look at the clock. It was 9:45 PM.

It's not even that late, he thought to himself.

The doors soon closed, and the train began moving. The clacking of the train's wheels along the track soothed him a bit, and he closed his eyes to relax until he reached his stop at the end of the line. A sudden wave of exhaustion took over him as he sat there, and within a few minutes, he dozed off.

———◆○◆———

The sound of the train's wheels clacking intensified, waking Jack from his sleep.

Oh shit, he thought as he pulled out his phone to check the time.

12:00AM

"How the fuck?" he said aloud.

Looking out the window of the train put him at even more unease. Instead of the subway walls and dim, yellow maintenance lights he should have seen, there was only blackness. It was as if the train had traveled into a void. He stared on, in disbelief, until movement in his peripheral pulled him out of his trance.

Turning his head forward, Jack gasped at the sight of a man in the next carriage staring at him through the window in the gangway door. With his bald, bulbous head and our-of-proportion features, the man looked like a caricature. His wide eyes stared over his elongated nose at Jack with a crazed look, and his crooked smile only added to his creepiness.

Feeling uncomfortable making eye contact, Jack unlocked his phone and began mindlessly scrolling through his photos. He was disheartened at the lack of cell service and hoped it would return soon.

As he continued to swipe through his pictures, images he hadn't taken began to appear; Images of dingy subway walls with graffiti written on them, images of the subway tracks, and images too blurry to make out what they were. He froze at the sight of an image of him on the station escalator. In the background, he could see the distorted man standing about twenty or thirty feet behind him.

He scrolled again, the next image showing him waiting on the subway platform. Once again, the man was standing just far enough behind him to barely be seen.

With a gulp, Jack looked up at the distorted man. He was still staring at him, only now, he was nodding his head in affirmation. He lifted his hand and extended his finger, making a swiping motion on the glass.

Jack looked down at his phone again and swiped to the next picture. It was a shot of him sitting in his seat. It was taken from behind, and in the background, the distorted man could be seen in the gangway window.

Looking up again, Jack almost screamed at the sight of the distorted man clapping his hands with joy. Jack wanted to cry but did his best to play it cool. Eventually, the man stopped his joyous clapping and went back to staring, only now, his expression turned to one of surprise. Before Jack could wonder what that meant, he heard a squealing sound and felt the train begin to slow.

Once the train had come to a complete stop, the distorted man held his hand up to the window with all five fingers extended. As if doing a countdown, he slowly lowered each finger one by one. The train's doors opened just as the final finger went down.

Unsure of what to do, Jack stood up. The distorted man, still staring at him, began shaking his head, as if warning him not to do so.

He slowly began making his way to the open door. As he approached, all he could see through the door was a dark tunnel, its dirty brick walls barely lit by the interior lights of the train.

He took a few more steps and leaned forward, sticking his head out the door to get a better look. In each direction, it looked as if the train was never ending.

"What the fuck!" He said, taking a step back from the door.

When he looked to his left, the distorted man was still there at the window. Without moving his head, the distorted man shifted his eyes back and forth between Jack and the open door. His hand was up to his mouth, and he was miming biting his nails in fear.

"What? Is something out there?" He screamed at the distorted man.

The man slammed both of his hands on the window and began nodding, giving Jack a solemn look.

"What's out there?" He screamed.

The distorted man shrugged.

Jack approached the door again and took another look outside. Still, he saw nothing but the train and brick wall. He turned back to the window. The distorted man was gone.

"Where did you g-"

His question was cut off by the sound of a woman's voice.

"Hello?" the voice called out.

Jack looked out the door again and saw the silhouette of a woman a few cars down.

"Hey!" he called out.

The woman turned to face him. "Oh, thank God," she called out and began running towards him.

Jack jumped out of the train and began walking towards her. As he got closer, he saw that the woman was Phoebe.

"Jack?" she said, now just a few feet away from him.

"Oh... uh... hey."

"What happened to you earlier?" she asked.

"Look. I'm sorry. We can talk about that later, okay. There are more important things to worry about right now."

"Like what?" she asked, looking offended.

"Like why does this train seem to go on forever? Why has it been running for hours now without stopping? Why did it stop here? Where the fuck is here? Who was that creepy man with the distorted face?" With that last question, he gestured towards the train car he had just jumped from.

With a confused expression, Phoebe looked at the train car, then back to Jack. "What creepy man?"

"He's... he's gone now. I guess. He was just staring at me through the window."

"Are you feeling okay?" Phoebe asked, reaching her hand out to touch Jack's forehead.

"I'm fine," he said, swatting her hand away, "I just want to get home."

Phoebe deflated at this. Her shoulders began to tremble, and Jack could see that she was crying. "Why did you leave me there at the restaurant? I barely had enough money to cover the bill."

Jack sighed and put his hands behind his head. He turned around and took a step away, unable to face her as he answered. "Because I thought you were annoying, okay. You just kept talking and talking. You wouldn't shut up. I couldn't take it anymore, so when you got up to use the bathroom, I left."

He waited for her to respond but heard nothing.

"Look, I'll pay you back for the bill," he said, turning to face her again. "I'm sorr-"

She was gone.

"Where did you go?" he asked.

Suddenly, the train doors closed, and the wheels started moving.

"Wait! Stop!" Jack called out, but the train kept moving, picking up speed as it went.

Feeling defeated, Jack stepped back and leaned against the wall as he watched the seemingly never-ending train go by. Eventually, he could see the end of the train approaching. He let out a scream as it passed.

There, on the other side of the tracks, stood the distorted man. Below his distorted face, he was shirtless. Dirty and tattered multicolored pants sagged from his waist. In his hand, he held a bloody knife.

"You shouldn't have left me there, Jack," the distorted man said in Phoebe's voice.

"Is... is this hell?" Jack asked.

With a laugh, the distorted man approached him. As the cold metal of the knife pierced through Jack's skin, the man spoke in Phoebe's voice one last time, "Something like that."

This is Gnome. He insisted I add this bonus short story to this novella. I hope you enjoyed it, and whatever you do, don't piss him off!

Afterword

I can honestly say I've never had a story hit this fast and flow so well. A few days before I started this, I was on a ride along at my job. We were driving down a rough, dirt road in the middle of the woods when an emergency alert for high winds came on the radio. With that setting, as soon as I heard the beeps of the emergency alert, it gave me chills and the gears in my mind started going.

I ended up writing the first three chapters of this novella with the intent of it being a short story for an upcoming submission **. I was so proud of it and, the more I sat on it, the more I wanted to expand on it. In just two days, I had the story to over three times the size it had originally been. It all just flowed naturally like a movie playing out in my head.

I hope that you, dear reader, enjoy this story. If not, I appreciate you taking the time to read the words I've put on paper.

Until next time....

Jason Nickey

1/17/2024

**The anthology I was planning to submit this story is the upcoming Hootenanny Horrorshow by From The Ashes Press. RJ Roles, the man behind From The Ashes is not only a great storyteller, but he has a knack for getting amazing writers and stories in his anthologies. Be sure to check out one of his books or anthologies. You won't be sorry.

About the Author

Jason Nickey is a horror writer from Charleston, West Virginia. He is a newer writer and has mostly worked in short fiction. He is a lifelong fan of all things horror and can sometimes be found either cosplaying as Jason Voorhees or brushing his luscious beard. Links to his bigcartel store, amazon store, and other social media platforms can be found at https://linktr.ee/bibliobeard

Also By Jason Nickey

Novellas:

Wreckage

Jasper And The Appalachian Zombies

Road Hazards

Collections:

Static And Other Stories

Reckless Abandon

They Come From Within

Collaborations:

Hillbillies And Homicidal Maniacs (With Stuart Bray)

When The Mockingbird Sings (With Stuart Bray)

Sludge (With Stuart Bray and Chuck Nasty)

Anthology Appearances:

Head Blown (Merrill David)

Til Death (From The Ashes)

Books Of Horror: Volume 4 Part 1

Harvested (From The Ashes)

Made in the USA
Las Vegas, NV
07 April 2024

88360877R00079